You DON'T Want a UNiCORN!

Written by
Ame Dyckman

Illustrated by **Liz Climo**

LB

LITTLE, BROWN AND COMPANY
NEW YORK BOSTON

You were gonna wish for a unicorn, weren't you? Wishing for a unicorn is a

BIG MISTAKE!

Just step away and—

PLIP

Uh-oh.
Things are about to get—

Sure, having a unicorn *seems* fun—
at first.

All right, *super* fun.

But it's not worth it.
What you don't know is unicorns

SHED

and SCRATCH,

and no matter how hard you try . . .

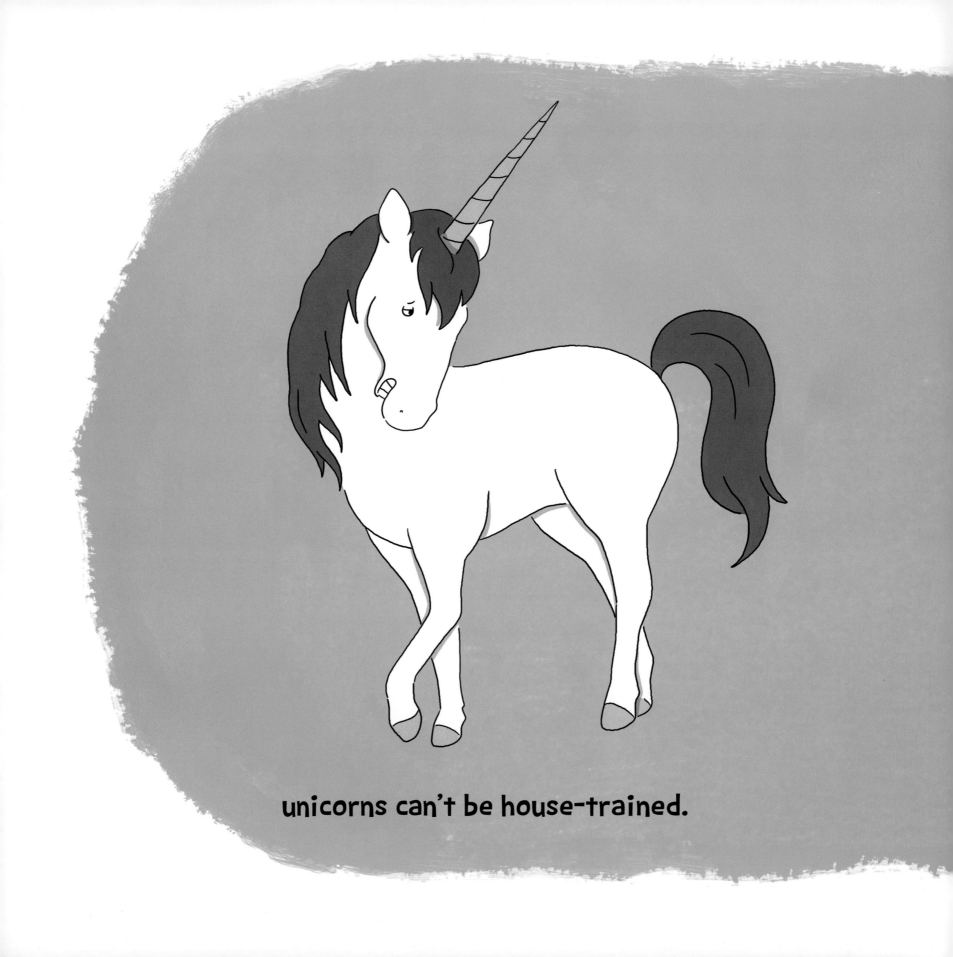

unicorns can't be house-trained.

Don't even get me started on

the **JUMPING,**

if it wasn't for the **biggest**, top secret,
nobody-knows-about-it problem
with having a unicorn:

Unicorns live in groups.
And when a unicorn gets lonely,

DING-
DING-
DING!

it calls a friend.

NO! Right when you're thinking this could be
double super fun–

POOF! There's **another.**

POOF!

And **another.**

Great. You've unleashed the
most destructive force
in the universe—

A UNICORN

PLIP

Aw, cheer up.
You could get a goldfish.
Or a nice rock.
Or—

Uh-oh.

STOP!

YOU DON'T WANT ONE OF *THOSE*, EITHER!

TRUST—

PLIP

me.

I ed unicorns. Still do. You never stop ♥ing unicorns—

even when they ruin your school's bake sale.

Trust me.

—Ame Dyckman

For Cooper, Kenley & Toby
—LC

For Adam. I always wanted an Adam.
But quit it with the cupcakes.
—AD

About This Book

The illustrations for this book were done with digital magic. The text was set in Barthowheel and the display type was hand-lettered by the illustrator. This book was edited by Mary-Kate Gaudet and designed by Jen Keenan with art direction by Saho Fujii. The production was supervised by Erika Schwartz, and the production editor was Marisa Finkelstein.